HERE and NOW

Words by Julia Denos
Illustrated by E. B. Goodale

HOUGHTON MIFFLIN HARCOURT • BOSTON • NEW YORK

Right here,
right now,

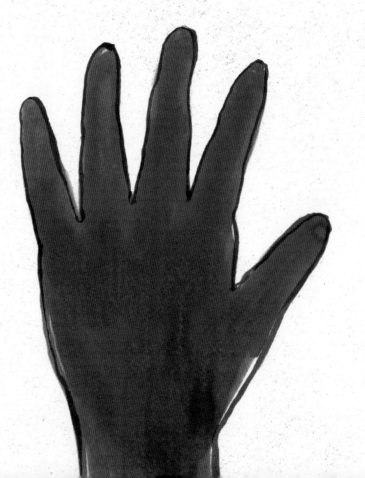

you are reading this book.

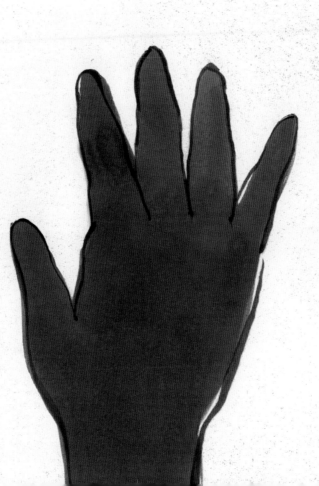

The book is in your lap,
or in your hands,
or in someone else's.

You are sitting,
or you are standing,
or you are wrapped up in a bed.

Under your bum, under your feet,
is a seat,
a floor . . .

. . . or a cloud (if you are on an airplane).

And under ALL of those things is the Earth.

the earthworms and the fossils,
the rocks.

And the Earth is spinning in the middle of space.
We don't know why.
But it is.

And you are too.

Right here,
right now,
while you are reading this book,
many, many things are happening:

Rain is forming in the belly of a cloud.

An ant has finished its home on the other side of the planet.

Somewhere, a telephone is ringing.

An idea is blooming..

Grass is pushing up through cement.

A friend you haven't met yet is sitting down to dinner.

There are animals,
wild ones
and tame,
living and breathing all around you.

Muscles are growing,

cities are growing,

babies are growing.

12

Cuts and broken bones are sewing up and healing.

Unseen work is being done.

Right here, right now,
YOU are becoming.

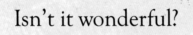

Isn't it wonderful?

AUTHOR'S NOTE

This book grew from
a poem I'd written called "In the Moment"
as part of my meditation practice. But instead of using
the traditional in-and-out breath, I used words and page turns
to help ground readers in their own moment—in that way, the book
is a real-time meditation.

Meditation is just another way of *noticing*, and noticing is a little bit
like magic. It brings us, *just as we are*, into the present moment, *just as it is*.
This freedom is a place I call "Here and Now." It is a land well known by young
children and plants and animals; it is a place where peace and possibility root, a
place where we feel connected to the greater unfolding story. Sometimes, when our
minds and bodies are busy, we forget how to get back. But all we need to do to
return again is to notice the world around us. We don't need to sit down, or
stop what we are doing. We don't even need to close our eyes.
Let's open our senses wide instead.

Right here, right now, you are done reading this book . . . but
the story hasn't ended! Like this moment, you are full of
every possibility. What will your story be as it
grows right from this spot, right
where you are?

For Ivy —J.D.

For George, Auriel, and Leo —E.B.G.

All rights reserved. For information about permission to reproduce selections from this book, write to
trade.permissions@hmhco.com or to Permissions, Houghton Mifflin Harcourt Publishing Company,
3 Park Avenue, 19th Floor, New York, New York 10016.

hmhco.com

The illustrations for this book were made using ink, watercolor, monoprinting, and digital collage.
The text type was set in Goudy Old Style.
The display type was set in Garden Grown.

Library of Congress Cataloging-in-Publication Data is on file.

ISBN: 978-1-328-46564-1

Manufactured in China
SCP 10 9 8 7 6 5 4 3 2 1
4500760850